Fat Magic

DE PAOLA

Fat Magic

BY
Steven Kroll

ILLUSTRATED BY
Tomie de Paola

HOLIDAY HOUSE • NEW YORK

For Bob Duffy
and for Mallory and Clarke Hambley

Text copyright © 1978 by Steven Kroll
Illustrations copyright © 1978 by Tomie de Paola
All rights reserved
Printed in the United States of America

Library of Congress Cataloging Publication Data
Kroll, Steven.
Fat magic.
SUMMARY: When the court magician puts a spell on
him that makes him grow very fat, Prince Timothy takes
some drastic measures to remedy the situation.
[1. Magic—Fiction. 2. Humorous stories]
I. De Paola, Thomas Anthony. II. Title.
PZ7.K9225Fat   [E]   77-28736
ISBN 0-8234-0327-0

It was a sunny winter afternoon. Prince Timothy was out on the top limb of his favorite tree. He was thinking about dessert.

Ice cream sundaes floated through his mind. So did chocolate layer cake and butterscotch pudding and sugar doughnuts.

Just as he was thinking about a trayful of chocolate éclairs, Edgar, the court magician, appeared.

"Hi," said Edgar. "You missed magic class yesterday."

"I did?" said Timothy. "Oh. I guess I forgot."

"Too much pie and pastry on your mind, I bet."

"No!" said Timothy, lying. "That's not true!"

"Sure it is. Everyone knows you never think about anything else."

"You just stop it, Edgar. You and your big feet!"

Edgar looked down at his big feet. "For that," he said, "I'm going to put a spell on you!"

And he waved his hand in the air and disappeared.

A moment later, Timothy began to feel himself growing fatter. He grew fatter. And fatter. And fatter.

Then the limb he was sitting on broke, and he
tumbled to the ground, making a huge hole.

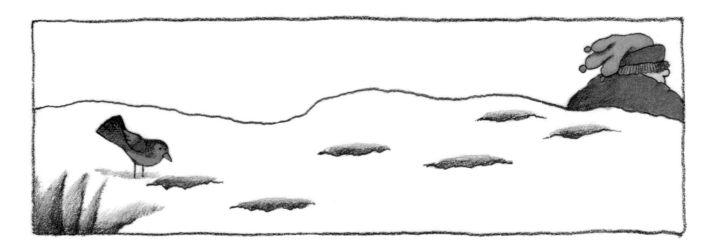

Timothy climbed out of the hole, grumbling. He
walked away, leaving gaping footprints behind him.

Timothy walked over to the royal skating pond.

Princess Melissa was doing pirouettes out in the middle.

Prince Basil was whizzing around the edge.

Timothy watched Melissa and Basil for a while.

Then he put on his skates, pushed off onto the ice ...

and promptly sank to the bottom of the pond.

Melissa and Basil skated over.

They tried to pull him out, but he was much too heavy.

"Why are you so fat?" asked Melissa.

"It was Edgar," said Timothy. "He put a spell on me."

"I bet," said Basil. "Probably too many chocolate éclairs. Everyone knows ——"

"Will you be quiet?" said Timothy. "And get me out of here?"

Basil and Melissa ran and found the king. The king came to the edge of the hole. "Why Timothy," he said, "what are you doing in there?"

"I fell through the ice."

"Oh dear," said the king. "I see." And he tried to pull Timothy out of the hole.

But Timothy wouldn't budge.

"Goodness," said the king. "This is terrible. You must go on a diet."

"I want to go inside," said Timothy, feeling very cold and wet. "Will you please get me out of here!"

"Oh, yes," said the king. "Why of course."

The king went and fetched the palace giant.

The giant leaned way out over the ice, picked up Timothy, and dumped him on the ground, where he made another huge hole.

"Thank you," said Timothy from the hole.

"You're welcome," said the giant, tipping his cap.

On the way up to the palace, Timothy left more gaping footprints behind him. When he reached the middle of the drawbridge, it collapsed.

"I don't know," said the king as he pulled Timothy from the moat. "I just don't know. What's your mother going to say about this?"

Climbing the palace stairs, Timothy had to go very slowly. When he reached the top, the queen came rushing out into the hall.

"Let me look at you!" she said. "What has happened to you?"

"Nothing, Mother," said Timothy. "Nothing, really."

"Oh, my baby! My poor, fat baby!"

"I think I'd better change out of my clothes," said Timothy.

But when he tried on some other clothes, they just didn't fit. He was simply too fat.

So he went to dinner in his royal cape.

Prince Basil, Princess Melissa, and the king and queen were waiting.

Timothy sat down in his chair, and it collapsed.

"Goodness," said the king. "You really must be more careful."

Timothy ate his dinner standing up.

He was served a partridge wing, three peas, and a very small boiled potato.

"Don't eat too much, dear," said the queen.

Timothy spent the evening in his room, thinking about jars full of cookies and feeling hungry.

The hungrier he got, the angrier he became. "That Edgar," he muttered to himself. "I'd like to squash him in his sleep!"

Quietly he opened his door. The palace was very still.
He tiptoed down the hall.

Timothy listened outside Edgar's door. He heard
nothing. Slowly he turned the knob.

Edgar was fast asleep. His big bare feet hung over the end of the bed.

Timothy squeezed through the door. As he crept toward the bed, he tripped over Edgar's fancy shoes.

There was a blinding flash and a blaze of light.
Edgar sat up. "Oh, no!" he yelled. "Not my shoes!
Don't take my magic shoes!"

"Aha!" said Timothy. "It's your shoes that make
your magic!"

He squeezed his toes into the silky, fancy shoes.
Timothy waved his hand over his head and thought
thin. Instantly, he was thin again. He waved his hand
at Edgar and thought fat. Instantly, Edgar was very
fat.

The bed sank swiftly to the floor.

"All right," said Edgar. "You've paid me back. What are you going to do now?"

"I think I'll keep you fat," said Timothy. "At least for a while." And he marched out of Edgar's room wearing the fancy shoes.

At breakfast the next morning, the royal family
watched Timothy change his orange juice into pop-
sicles, his cereal into jelly beans, and his milk into a
vanilla ice cream soda.

"I don't understand," said the king. "You're not so fat any more, and you're making magic."

"It's the shoes," said Timothy. "I'm wearing Edgar's magic shoes."

"I see," said the king. "And how does Edgar feel about that?"

"He's very fat," said Timothy. "At least for a while." Then he ran out of the dining room and down the palace stairs to begin a perfect morning.

He changed some snow into salt water taffy and ate
it. He grew some chocolate apples on the royal apple
trees.

He changed some stones into cherry cupcakes and a
fence into peanut brittle, and he didn't give Basil and
Melissa any, not even when they asked him.

But while Timothy was having so much fun in Edgar's shoes, Edgar himself was miserable. First he got wedged in his bedroom doorway.

Next, he caught a cold from wandering around barefoot.

Then his horse fell down when he tried to get on, and
he rolled into the royal garden, where he squashed
the queen's prize rosebushes. By mid-afternoon, Edgar
was one very unhappy magician.

The king and queen were not very happy either.
Edgar was supposed to set a good example. Timothy
simply had to give back the magic shoes.

"Sure I will," said Timothy over afternoon tea. "But
on one condition."

"What's that?" asked the king and queen.

"I can eat whatever I want whenever I want, without
being teased."

The king choked on his cake. The queen spilled her
tea. But they agreed.

Then Timothy went and found Edgar.

"I've come to give you back your shoes," he said.

"Oh, really?" said Edgar. "What's the trick?"

"No trick," said Timothy. "Just stop teasing me about sweets."

"All right," said Edgar. "But will you take back what you said about my feet?"

"Why not?" said Timothy. Then he waved his hand in the air, and Edgar became his normal size.

Timothy handed over the fancy shoes.

"Thank you," said Edgar.

"You're welcome," said Timothy. "But you still have the longest nose I've ever seen!"

Edgar's mouth dropped open. "I'm moving to another kingdom," he said. "I've had enough."

"Bye," said Timothy, watching him go.

Then he dashed off to the palace kitchen to raid the royal icebox.